The Strongest Animal

by Janice Boland

pictures by Gary Torrisi

Richard C. Owen Publishers, Inc.
Katonah, New York

On Sunday I went to the zoo.

I saw the biggest elephant.

I saw the tallest giraffe.

I saw the funniest monkey.

I saw the fiercest lion.

He roared at me

and I dropped my potato chip.

Then I saw the strongest animal of all, a tiny ant!

It picked up my potato chip,

and carried it away.